Maya's Magic Carpet

By Michelle Zellers

Illustrated by Mary Wilcop

WE READ assisted by MarketingNewAuthors.com of Ann Arbor, MI

Copyright © 2006

Printed In China

ISBN: 1-889743-48-8

2005-2006

The publication and donation of this book was made possible by:

University of Michigan's Summer Student Assembly
Michigan Student Assembly's Budgetary Priorities Committee
LSA Student Government's Budgetary Allocations Committee
The Edward Ginsberg Center for Community Service and Learning

WE READ would also like to thank the following people
without whose help this would not have been possible:

Fairy Hayes-Scott
Steve Gee

Nick Tobier
Susan Parrish
Laura Roop

WE READ Coordinating Board:
Keith Fudge, Willa Tracosas, Andrea Lubaway, Tegan Gifford,
Lauren Deaton, Preeti Samudra, Eunice Ko

WE READ Editors:
Amy Geppert, Hayley Gollub, Heather Guith, Miriam Levine,
Rebecca Soares, Sara Tumen, Andrea Vought

Our mission is to promote interest and enthusiasm in reading by offering opportunities for
students to engage in reading and its related activities.

WE READ (Working to Educate Readers by Encouraging Active Development)

In the country of Spain, in the heart of Madrid
Lived a friendly, adventurous, kind-hearted kid.
She would dream every night
Of the land beyond sight
As she lay down to sleep in her bed.

On ten birthday candles, she wished for a glance
At Italy, Kenya, Australia, and France.
But little she knew
That her wish would come true—
That she soon would be given that chance.

A world map was stitched on the rug in bright thread—
The oceans in blue and the mountains in red.
It was truly a sight,
But soon would come night,
So she put it down and got into bed.

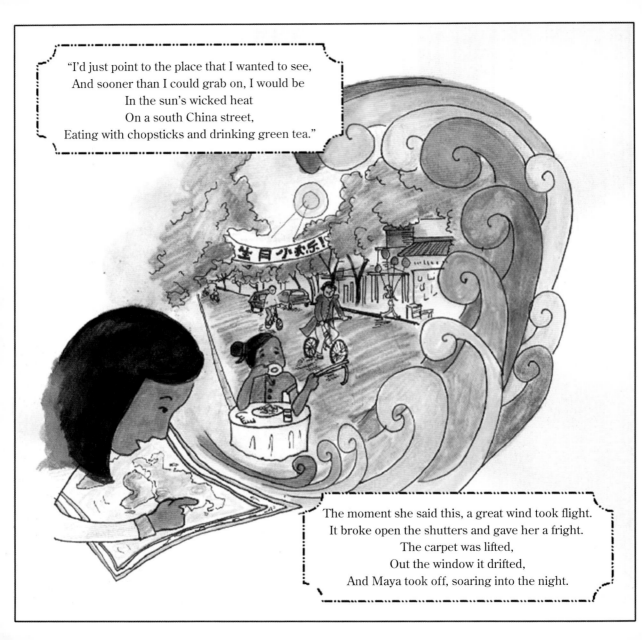

"I'd just point to the place that I wanted to see,
And sooner than I could grab on, I would be
In the sun's wicked heat
On a south China street,
Eating with chopsticks and drinking green tea."

The moment she said this, a great wind took flight.
It broke open the shutters and gave her a fright.
The carpet was lifted,
Out the window it drifted,
And Maya took off, soaring into the night.

With the wind at her back and the moon on her face,
Maya felt she could fly at a hurricane's pace.
She could sail through the clouds
And look down at the crowds,
Overcome any obstacle, go any place.

And it seemed that in no time, Maya was there,
Traveling with ease through the cool Paris air.
Touring, exploring—
Not a moment was boring!
For now she could journey wherever she dared.

Sure enough, Maya made use of this power,
Wandering about for nearly an hour—
Seeing the sights
And the bright city lights,
The Arc de Triomphe and the great Eiffel Tower.

Then, she thought to herself, "It would be very nice
If I had a local to give me advice
On places to go
And would make sure I know
What's not worth my time and what's worth seeing twice."

Nearby, a child looked down at the land,
Holding a flashlight in the palm of her hand.
When the little girl slept,
Like Maya she dreamt
To travel wherever her heart would command.

Now, the girl thought that stories of carpets that flew
Were just make-believe and were not really true.
But to her surprise,
Right before her own eyes
Were a magical rug and a little girl, too.

So her lips formed a smile, and her eyes began gleaming;
She covered her mouth to prevent her own screaming.
Her heart started racing;
Her feet kept on pacing,
And being awake felt no different than dreaming.

Unlatching the window and climbing aboard,
Adrienne sent the tapestry lingering toward
The stars and the moon
Like a hot air balloon,
And above the horizon they leisurely soared.

So, together the girls flew around for a while
Seeing town after town, seeing mile after mile.
After much exploration
In Adrienne's nation,
The girl turned to Maya and said with a smile:

"You've seen so many things on this magical day
From cathedrals and mountains to famous cafés.
You've explored high and low
And learned facts you should know,
But you haven't seen France till you've seen the ballet!"

Then, quicker than lightning she drove through the air
With a flame in her heart and a breeze in her hair.
But her eyes formed a tear
As the theater drew near,
And the look on her face was a look of despair.

Determined to see a performance that day,
They circled the building and looked for a way.
Maya thought they could soar
Through the staff member door,
And soon the two children were in the ballet.

And the tapestry floated backstage in mid-air—
Not a person in sight even knew they were there.
They just sat there in awe
Of the dancer they saw
With pink shoes on her feet and a rose in her hair.

Then, the theater was hushed, and the curtain arose,
Revealing the girl who was striking a pose.
When the orchestra played
And the music was made,
She started to dance on the tips of her toes.

So, they silently watched as she leaped and she pranced
'Cause she seemed to be telling a tale as she danced.
And she moved with such grace
That she dazzled the place,
And in less than an instant, the crowd was entranced.

Now, the audience truly could not ask for more,
But soon other ladies were taking the floor.
They twirled, and they spun,
And they all moved as one,
And they danced just as well as the dancer before.

Maya loved the ballet, and she wished it would last,
But quickly a couple of hours had passed.
When the curtain had closed,
Maya supposed
That something so wonderful goes by too fast.

And with that the explorers set off in the sky.
Back to Adrienne's window the carpet did fly.
She had been a great guide,
And they had a fun ride,
But both the girls knew it was time for goodbye.

Maya said "Adios" as she left Adrienne,
And she hoped she'd be able to see her again.
She had fun at the dance,
And she loved seeing France,
But the best part was getting to meet a new friend.

"Time to go home," Maya said with a sigh,
But she got a bit tired on her trip through the sky.
Then, her eyes started closing,
And soon she was dozing,
But somehow the tapestry knew where to fly.

And into her bedroom it magically flew
As she dreamed of the marvelous things she would do.
She would visit new places
While meeting new faces,
So surely the little girl's dream had come true!